Ayedin Learns to Share

Written By: Keisha Cameron

Illustrated by: Artem H

From the Ayedin Learns Series

This book belongs to

_____

_____

_____

For Kadeem, Malia, Kal-El and Ayedin.
It is always wonderful to see how you are all
growing and learning amazing things.

Dear reader,

One of the most amazing things about being a parent is passing on little pockets of wisdom to our children.

We teach them to say "Thank you," "Please," "Good morning," and even the importance of sharing.

This book was written based on a learning and teaching experience I had with my son, Ayedin, that we want to share with you.

We hope you will be able to use the gems learnt from this book, especially that sometimes sharing does not mean giving away the extra that you have; but enjoying what you have with someone else.

Sincerely

Ayedin's Mommy

It was a beautiful and sunny day.

Ayedin wanted to visit the park so he could play with his soccer ball.

He jumped out of bed, ran to mommy and asked, "Mommy, can we go to the park, please?"

Mommy looked up at the clock to check the time. She smiled at him.

"Sure, Ayedin, let's get our shoes and you can grab your ball."

They put on their shoes and Ayedin took up his soccer ball which was his favorite color. BLUE!

Ayedin smiled as he and mommy held hands and happily strolled to the park. He couldn't wait to play soccer with his favorite blue ball.

Ayedin also liked visiting the park so he could see all the people doing different activities there.
There were lots of fun games and activities at the park. There were swings, slides, a riding trail, and even an area to play soccer.

Kal-El was also at the park and he rode his shiny new bike.
His new bike was painted in his favorite color. **BLUE!**
Kal-El laughed as it was lots of fun to ride his bike.

As soon as Ayedin saw Kal-El, he ran over to him, stopped, and stared at his bike. He was amazed.

He immediately wanted to try riding this shiny **BLUE** bike.
After all, it was blue, and riding a bike seemed
to be lots of fun.

Ayedin was too shy to ask Kal-El to share his bike, so he continued to stare.
Kal-El's mom smiled, "Hi, Ayedin, would you like to try?"

Ayedin tugged on mommy's shirt and barely raised his voice, "Mommy, can I try?" "You have to ask Kal-El and don't forget to say please." She gently nudged him towards Kal-El with a smile.

Ayedin looked at Kal-El and asked,
"Can I try, please?"
Kal-El held on tightly to his bike handles and scrunched up his nose, "No!"

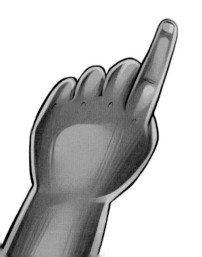

Kal-El also wanted to play with Ayedin's soccer ball. After all, it was also his favorite color and Kal-El loved playing soccer.
"Mommy, can I play with his soccer ball, please?"
Ayedin held on to his soccer ball and scrunched up his nose, "No!"

"Sharing is caring, Ayedin, you have to share your soccer ball and Kal-El will share his bike," Ayedin's mommy said encouragingly.

"That's right, boys, you can take turns riding the bike and then play soccer together. That way it's a lot more fun," Kal-El's mommy added.

Both Ayedin and Kal-El started thinking that their mommies were right and then said, "Okay." Ayedin tossed his soccer ball towards Kal-El and said, "Here."

Kal-El pushed his bike towards Ayedin and said,
"Lets share."

The two boys started laughing and enjoying themselves and soon realized it was way more fun when they shared their toys.

They both took turns riding Kal-El's bike and then played soccer with Ayedin's ball.

Soon it was time to go
home and everyone
had so much fun.
They happily waved
goodbye.
"See you tomorrow!"

"Wasn't that fun, Ayedin? You got to play with two toys instead of one. It's always more fun when you share."
"Yes, mommy! And we both love the color blue!"

Mommy felt really proud that Ayedin learned to share his toy and had so much fun doing so.

"We should definitely try sharing more often, right, Ayedin? There are lots of other stuff you can share," mommy said to Ayedin as they walked home.

Coloring Activity

Hey, Kids,

There are so many ways to share

You can share your toys on the playground.
You can share your toys when you have friends over at your house.
You can share your snacks, books, pencils and crayons with friends at school.
You can share your storybooks with your family.

**Always remember, to show you care,
it's nice to share**

Made in the USA
Middletown, DE
11 December 2021

55204705R00020